FAVOURITE STORIES

HarperCollins *Children's Books*

Contents

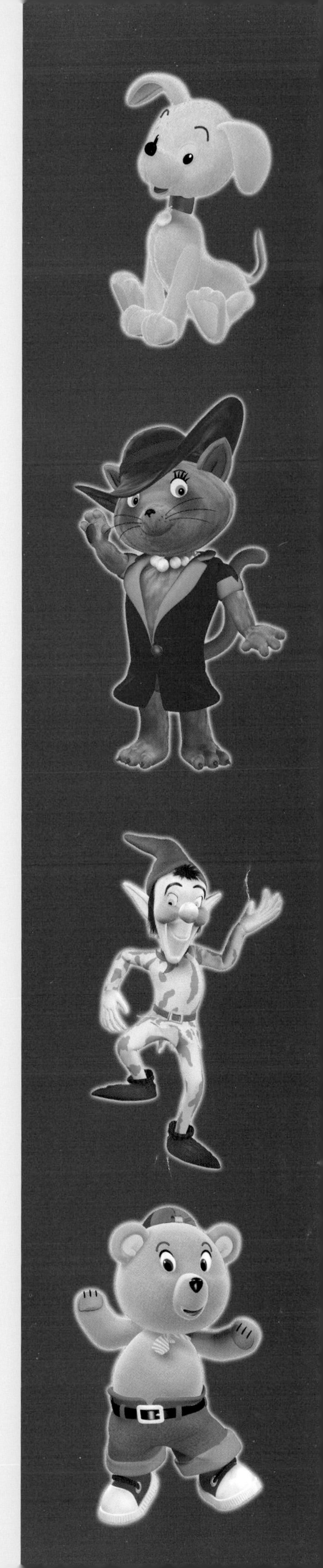

Noddy's Perfect Gift

It was a peaceful morning in Toy Town, until…

VROOM! Noddy's little yellow car roared up the road and screeched to a halt outside Toadstool House.

Noddy jumped out, pushed open the front door and dashed inside.

"Big-Ears! Big-Ears!" he shouted.

“It must be very important if you’re in such a rush, Noddy,” said Big-Ears. “What’s the problem?”

“I don’t know! I don’t know! I don’t know!” cried Noddy, pacing up and down.

“Well, if you don’t know what the problem is, how can I possibly help you?” said Big-Ears.

Noddy tried to explain.

"Oh, Big-Ears, I'm not sure if my birthday present for Tessie Bear is enough. It's just a song I made up."

"A song sounds like a lovely present, Noddy," said Big-Ears smiling. "Sing it and I'll tell you what I think."

Noddy cleared his throat and began to sing:

This song is for your birthday, Tessie Bear, it's true.
Yes, every note I've written is especially for you.
I like you, Tessie Bear, you must know it's true.
Friend of mine, every line shows how much I do.

"What do you think, Big-Ears?" Noddy asked. "Should it be longer? Shorter? Prettier?"

"It's perfect just as it is, Noddy," said Big-Ears.

"Are you sure, Big-Ears?" said Noddy.

"She'll love it, Noddy," Big-Ears promised him. "Off you go, now! And don't come back until you've sung it to her."

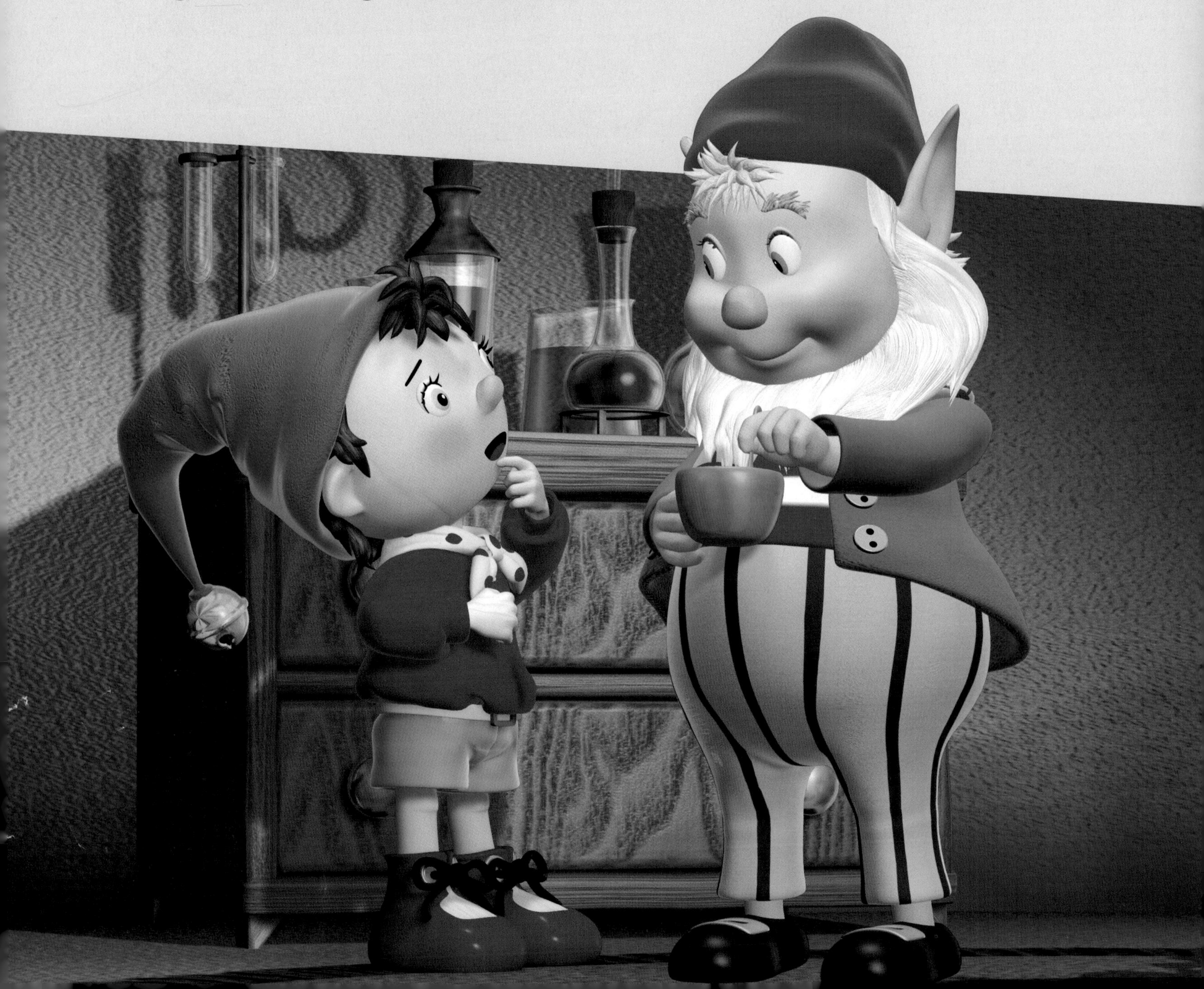

Noddy set off to see Tessie Bear.

Suddenly someone called out, “Taxi! Taxi!” It was Martha Monkey. Noddy pulled over.

“Sorry Martha, I can’t give you a lift, I’ve got something very important to do!”

But Martha just jumped in. “Oh, please, Noddy, I need to get to Town Square.”

“OK then,” sighed Noddy.

"I hear it's Tessie Bear's birthday," said Martha, when they arrived in Toy Town. "Is she having a party? Who's invited? And, most important, what are you giving her?"

"A song! I made it up myself," said Noddy.

"A song is nice, I suppose," said Martha, "but it might not be enough to make her feel *extra* special."

Noddy looked worried again. Perhaps a song wasn't the best present, after all.

"Oh, Martha," he cried. "What *would* make Tessie Bear feel extra special?"

"Flowers always make *me* feel special," said Martha giving him a wink.

"Of course! Flowers!" Noddy whooped happily. "Why didn't I think of that?"

Noddy was sure Tessie Bear would like the forget-me-nots he'd bought. They were just like the flowers on her hat.

"What lovely flowers," said Mr Wobbly Man.

"They're for Tessie Bear," Noddy told him proudly. "And I've made up a special birthday song for her."

"Lucky Tessie!" said Mr Wobbly Man. "But what about a cake? A cake is the best part of a birthday."

"Oh, no! I didn't think of that," wailed Noddy. "I've just got time to make one. Will you help me?"

Whirrrrrrrrr… went the mixing machine.

"Phew! Whipping up a cake is hard work," said Noddy.

"Let me taste it for you," said Mr Wobbly Man, scooping some of the creamy mixture into his mouth.

"Hmmm. This cake mixture needs a little more… tasting!" said Mr Wobbly Man and he gobbled it all up!

“Sorry, Noddy, you’ll have to make another one,” said Mr Wobbly Man.

“But I’ve only got enough eggs for a bite-sized cake, this time,” moaned Noddy. “No more tasting, Mr Wobbly Man!” he said firmly, measuring more flour into his mixing bowl.

"Small but perfect," said Noddy proudly as he took the cake out of the oven. "And it smells scrumptious."

"Shall I have a little taste, just to make sure?" suggested Mr Wobbly Man.

"No!" cried Noddy, snatching the cake away. "I'm taking it to Tessie Bear, right now!"

But Mr Wobbly Man started to groan. "Ooo, my tummy! I've eaten too much cake mixture."

Poor Noddy had to drive Mr Wobbly Man to the shop to get some medicine. Would he ever get to Tessie Bear's house?

As he came out of the shop, Noddy saw Sly and Gobbo, the two goblins, leaning over his car.

"Hey!" Noddy shouted. "What are you up to?"

The naughty goblins jumped back.

"We were, er… you tell him, Sly," said Gobbo.

"Me?" said Sly. "Oh, OK. We were trying to snatch –"

SLAP! Gobbo slapped a hand over Sly's mouth and hissed, "*Sniff* not *snatch*. We were just sniffing the pretty flowers. The cake smelt yummy, too."

Noddy rushed to his car. The cake and flowers were safe. “Those are my presents for Tessie’s birthday,” he told the goblins.

“Birthday presents, eh?” said Gobbo thoughtfully. "We can help with presents, can’t we, Sly?”

And he yanked Sly aside to whisper to him. There was a lot of giggling and Sly kept nodding his head.

Finally, the two cheeky goblins turned back to Noddy. Gobbo said, “Sly and I think the best way to make Tessie Bear happy is to give her…”

“…some jelly!” sniggered Sly.

“No!” hissed Gobbo. “Jewellery!”

“Jewellery?” said Noddy, looking worried.

“Yes and we know where you can get it,” said Gobbo.

"Step this way for some wonderful jewellery," said Gobbo, hurrying Noddy down a back street.

"Are you sure there's a jewellery shop here?" said Noddy, wondering if he should trust them.

"Oh, yes," said Sly. "Look!"

"What? Where? In these boxes?" gasped Noddy.

“This box is full of jewellery,” said Gobbo, trying not to giggle. “Look! You’ll be surprised.”

Noddy thought it might be a trick but he just couldn’t help peeping into the box.

Quick as a flash, Sly and Gobbo pushed him in and shut the lid. Poor Noddy was trapped!

“Yep! He was surprised, all right,” chortled Sly.

“Now for the great car snatch!” yelled Gobbo.

The goblins raced down the street and dived into Noddy’s car. Shrieking with laughter, they roared up and down the road, beeping the horn.

PARP! PARP!

And, to tease poor Noddy, they gave an extra loud beep every time they passed.

THUNK. THUNK. THUNK. The box bumped angrily down the street.

Then, just as Mr Plod walked by, the box suddenly jumped!

"Aghh!" the policeman shouted in surprise.

A loud knocking came from inside the box. Mr Plod crept closer to have a look.

All at once, the box burst open and up popped Noddy! He was very cross.

"Arrest them, Mr Plod," he cried. "They're stealing my car!"

"Who? What? Where?" gasped Mr Plod, looking all around.

Just then, the goblins came roaring down the road in Noddy's little car.

"Why, those scoundrels!" said Mr Plod. He stepped into the road, raised his hand and blew a loud blast on his whistle.

"PEEEEP! Stop in the name of Plod!" he commanded.

Gobbo braked hard. The little yellow car screeched to a halt, only just missing Mr Plod.

The two goblins bashed their noses on the windscreen. “Aghh! Ouch!” they groaned.

“You ought to be ashamed of yourselves, stealing Noddy’s car like that,” Mr Plod told them sternly.

"Sorry, Mr Plod," said Gobbo. "Sometimes our naughty side just runs away with us!"

"Yeah, like now!" yelled Sly. And the two naughty goblins leaped out of the car and ran away, hooting with laughter. Mr Plod raced off after them, blowing his whistle. PEEEP-PEEP!

Poor Noddy. His cake and flowers were crushed to bits.

"What's the matter, Noddy?" asked Big-Ears, who was passing by.

"I wanted to give Tessie an *extra*-special birthday. But Sly and Gobbo have wrecked everything," cried Noddy.

"But what about your song? It came straight from your heart," said Big-Ears. "It's a perfect present!"

"You really think so?" said Noddy. And he rushed off to find Tessie.

This song is for your birthday, Tessie Bear, it's true.

Yes, every note I've written is especially for you.

I like you, Tessie Bear, you must know it's true.

Friend of mine, every line shows how much I do.

Noddy stopped singing and looked shyly at Tessie.

"Thank you, Noddy!" She beamed at him.

"It's the most perfect present I've ever had!"

A Bike for Big-Ears

It was a sunny morning in Toy Town…

Noddy was driving carefully, as usual. But on this particular day he had a very tricky passenger in his car.

"Don't put me off while I'm driving," he told Clockwork Clown, "or we'll have a crash."

"Who, me? I wouldn't dream of it, Noddy," grinned Clockwork Clown.

Noddy stopped at the road junction just outside Toy Town.

Ting-a-ling-a-ling! Big-Ears rang his bell as he cycled past.

"Big-Ears must be going into Toy Town to buy something at Dinah Doll's stall," said Noddy.

Clockwork Clown wasn't listening. With a grin, he took out a shiny, red balloon and – BANG! – he popped it! It gave Noddy a real fright.

"Aghh!" he yelled and, by mistake, he put his foot down on the accelerator. Before he knew what had happened, the car was skidding crazily through the streets of Toy Town.

Noddy struggled to stop his car. “Phew! That wasn’t very nice,” he gasped.

But just as Noddy turned to ask Clockwork Clown why he’d played such a silly trick, the clown leaped up and did a somersault over the windscreen.

“Thanks for the ride, Noddy!” he grinned.

Noddy was very upset. He'd almost had a crash thanks to that balloon!

"I *do* drive carefully," he said to himself as he drove on, "but it's difficult with clowns like that in the car. I'm a *good* driver..."

CRRUNNNCH!

"Uh-oh! I've hit something!" cried poor Noddy.

"Oh, no!" groaned Big-Ears, who had been talking to Dinah Doll. "My beautiful bike! You've crushed it!"

"I'm so sorry, Big-Ears! I'm really, really sorry!" cried Noddy.

"They don't make bikes like that any more," moaned Big-Ears, looking at his smashed bike.

"Don't worry, Big-Ears," said Noddy. "I'll take it to Mr Sparks. He'll know what to do."

"Noddy's right, Big-Ears," said Dinah Doll. "If anyone can fix it, Mr Sparks can."

Noddy's face lit up. "And he could add some new things," he said. "A big horn, or flashing lights, or..."

"No horns. No flashing lights," said Big-Ears, firmly.

"But Big-Ears..." cried Noddy.

"No, Noddy. I don't want anything new. My bike was perfect just as it was."

"Oh, all right," said Noddy.

Noddy took Big-Ears' bike to the Toy Town garage.

"Can you fix it, Mr Sparks?" he asked.

"Of course, Noddy, I'll make it as good as new."

"I bet you could make it even better!" said Noddy. "But Big-Ears wants his old bike back just as it was."

"Some people don't like change," said Mr Sparks.

"I feel bad about wrecking his bike, Mr Sparks," said Noddy. "Is there any way you could make it better than it was?"

"Hmm," said Mr Sparks. "Ah-ha, I do have an idea, Noddy. I could fit Big-Ears' bike with a motor."

"Oh, *yes*, Mr Sparks!" Noddy was thrilled. "A motor would make his bike much more fun."

"Can you hide the motor in this basket?" Noddy asked. "Then Big-Ears'll get a real surprise when he starts pedalling."

"Fitting a motor in a basket is quite a challenge," said Mr Sparks, "...but I like it!" And he rolled up his sleeves and got started.

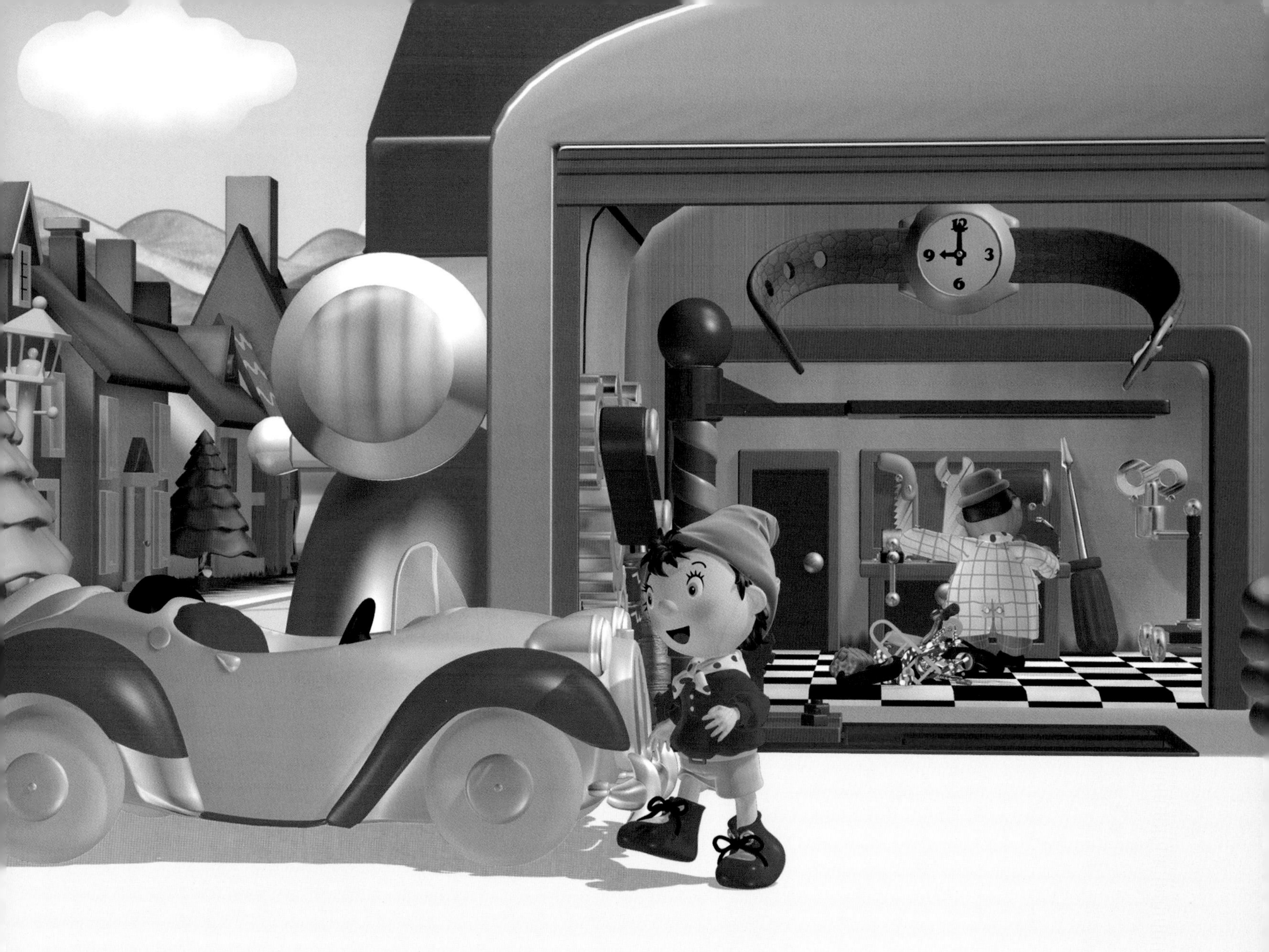

Happy now, Noddy skipped out of the garage, singing:

Count on me, any time at all,
I will always answer when you call.
Count on me, I will see you through,
And I know that I can count on you!

Later, Noddy took the mended bike to Big-Ears at Toadstool House.

"Here it is, Big-Ears," said Noddy, proudly.

"Ahh!" Big-Ears gasped. "It's beautiful! Thank you, Noddy. But what's this? I thought I asked you not to add anything new."

"It's only a basket, Big-Ears, and..."

"I love it, Noddy! It's what I've always wanted," said Big-Ears, smiling.

"It's a special kind of basket, Big-Ears," Noddy started to explain. "To make you go faster!"

"You are funny, Noddy," Big-Ears chuckled. "A basket can't make my bike go any faster!"

"Just try it!" said Noddy, eagerly.

"If Mr Sparks fixed my bike, I'm sure it's as good as new, Noddy," said Big-Ears.

"It's *better* than new, Big-Ears. Much better!" cried Noddy.

"You're right, Noddy," said Big-Ears as he began to pedal his bike. "Mr Sparks did a great job."

He rode slowly around Noddy.

"Faster, Big-Ears. Pedal faster!" cried Noddy.

"All right, I will," said Big-Ears.

"Thundering toadstools! It's ALIVE!" cried poor Big-Ears as his pedalling kick-started the motor-in-a-basket.

"Aaghh!" he shrieked as the bike roared away. "Watch out, Noddy. I can't stop! HELP!"

Big-Ears tried his best to steer, but his bike was going too fast. It swerved around Noddy and zoomed off down the road towards Toy Town, with Big-Ears clinging on for dear life.

Noddy jumped into his little car and tore after Big-Ears.

"Quick, little car, we've got to rescue Big-Ears!" cried Noddy, chasing after the runaway bike.

As Noddy raced along, he shouted, "Slow down, Big-Ears!"

"I caaaaaaan't!" yelled Big-Ears.

Big-Ears, on the runaway bike, hurtled past Clockwork Clown.

Then Noddy whizzed by.

"Whooahh!" Clockwork Clown was whirled round by the whoosh of air from the car.

"Oops! Sorry!" yelled Noddy. "Can't stop!"

"Any minute now," cried Noddy in a panic, "we'll be in the middle of Toy Town's busy streets!"

Ting-a-ling-a-ling! Big-Ears rang his bell madly, warning everyone to get out of his way.

"Sorry!" he shouted as he shot past Mr Wobbly Man and sent him spinning across the road.

"Look out! Coming through!" Big-Ears yelled as he bounced off a rubbish bin, ran over a little tree, then whizzed past Clockwork Mouse, Mr Jumbo, Dinah Doll and Tessie Bear.

"Looks like Mr Sparks got that bike working a little *too* well," said Dinah Doll.

At top speed, Big-Ears roared straight into Mr Sparks' open garage.

CRASH! BANG! BUMP! THUMP! CRUNCH!

Tools, bits and pieces of cars and bikes flew through the air as Big-Ears smashed into the workshop – and out again.

“Help!” wailed Big Ears. “I can’t hold on much longer!”

Noddy had to do something – and fast!

He drove up behind his old friend, yelling, “When I say, ‘Now!’ Big-Ears, jump into my car!”

“OK!” Big-Ears gasped. “Just get me off this thing!”

It wasn't easy to drive alongside the runaway bike, but Noddy managed it.

"Ready… NOW!" he shouted.

Big-Ears leaped off his bike – and into Noddy's car.

He was safe at last, thanks to Noddy's brave and clever driving. His bike zoomed straight into a wall. KERRUNCH!

Big-Ears' bike was smashed again. But at least the motor-in-a-basket had finally stopped.

"I'm sorry, Big-Ears. I wanted to make your bike better. So I asked Mr Sparks to put a motor on it."

"So I see, Noddy," said Big-Ears. "Next time you want to help someone, do what they ask for, not what you think is best for them!"

"I will," said Noddy. "I'll ask Mr Sparks to mend your bike just the way you like it."

Then Noddy grinned. "Are you *sure* you don't want any flashing lights, Big-Ears?" he asked.

"You funny little Noddy," said Big-Ears. "You know I don't."

And they both laughed until the bell on Noddy's hat jingled.

Noddy Goes Shopping

It was a peaceful morning in Toy Town…

PARP! PARP! The startled folk of Toy Town looked up as Noddy's car hurtled through the streets.

"We made it!" gasped Mrs Skittle as the car screeched to a halt at the station.

"Now, Noddy," she said. "How much do I owe you?"

Noddy wasn't sure.

"Um, did I say two children count as one grown up, or..."

"Noddy!" cried Mrs Skittle. "I don't have time for this. Here! Keep the change." And she dropped a heap of coins into his hand.

"Oh!" cried Noddy. "What a lot of money!"

Noddy jumped into his car and zoomed across town to Big-Ears' house.

"Hello, Big-Ears!" cried Noddy, running up the stairs. "I've just earned loads of money. We could go out and spend it on… oh!"

He stopped in surprise.

Big-Ears was still in bed!

"Big-Ears! It's the middle of the morning and you're still asleep!" said Noddy.

"I wish I *was* asleep," Big-Ears yawned, loudly. "That's the problem. I just can't seem to get to sleep at all."

"Then why don't you go to bed early?" suggested Noddy.

"I can't get to sleep!" said Big-Ears, crossly. "If I weren't so tired, I'd go into town to buy the things I need to make a sleeping charm."

"*I'll* go for you!" cried Noddy.

"That's very kind," said Big-Ears. "Now, listen: I'll need a small cloth bag to hold everything."

"Small cloth bag," repeated Noddy. "Got it."

"A bunch of night-blooming flowers to make me feel sleepy."

"OK," said Noddy. "What else?"

Big-Ears thought hard. “A small black stone, to make my eyes feel heavy.”

“Right,” said Noddy. “Small black stone.”

“And a few little white balls of cotton wool to use as ear plugs. Oh, yes, and a torch, to remind me of the calming moonlight.”

"You must remember all the things," said Big-Ears. "If you forget just one of them, the charm won't work."

"Don't worry, Big-Ears!" said Noddy.

Big-Ears yawned. "And I also need a toy saw," he said. "It'll get me snoring."

“Six things,” said Noddy, as he headed for the door. “I’ll remember all of them!”

Big-Ears checked the time. “Noddy should be back in about half an hour.”

And he settled back to wait.

One hour and forty-five minutes later, Noddy had still not come back.

"Where on earth *is* Noddy?" yawned Big-Ears. "He should be back by now."

The clock ticked away.

But still Noddy did not come back. Big-Ears grew more and more worried.

Just then, he heard the front door open, and the sound of eager footsteps coming up the stairs.

“I’m back!” cried Noddy, bursting into the room.
“What took you so long?” asked Big-Ears.
“Sorry,” said Noddy, dumping a large box on the floor. “It just took a while to get all six things.”

"Here's the cloth bag," said Noddy, pulling a large sack out of the box.

Big-Ears peered into it.

"I can't see any little bag. Are you sure it's in here?"

“It’s not *in* the sack,” laughed Noddy. “It *is* the sack!”

“Noddy,” groaned Big-Ears, “I said a *small* bag.”

“Oops!” said Noddy. “Does it matter? Surely, the bigger the better?”

Big-Ears sighed.

"What about the ear plugs?" asked Big-Ears.

Noddy handed Big-Ears some hard white balls.

"Oh, no! Not golf balls!" wailed Big-Ears. "I said *cotton wool* balls."

Noddy shrugged. "All I could remember was white balls. Sorry!"

Big-Ears shook his head. "Well, Noddy… did you remember the small black stone?"

Noddy pulled a big, grey rock out of the box.

"Honestly, Noddy," frowned Big-Ears. "I said a small black stone. This is big and grey!"

"Oh, dear. I forgot about the size," said Noddy, "but I didn't forget the colour!"

He pulled out a black pencil and started scribbling on the rock.

"Have you remembered *anything* properly?" moaned Big-Ears.

Noddy put his hand back into the box.

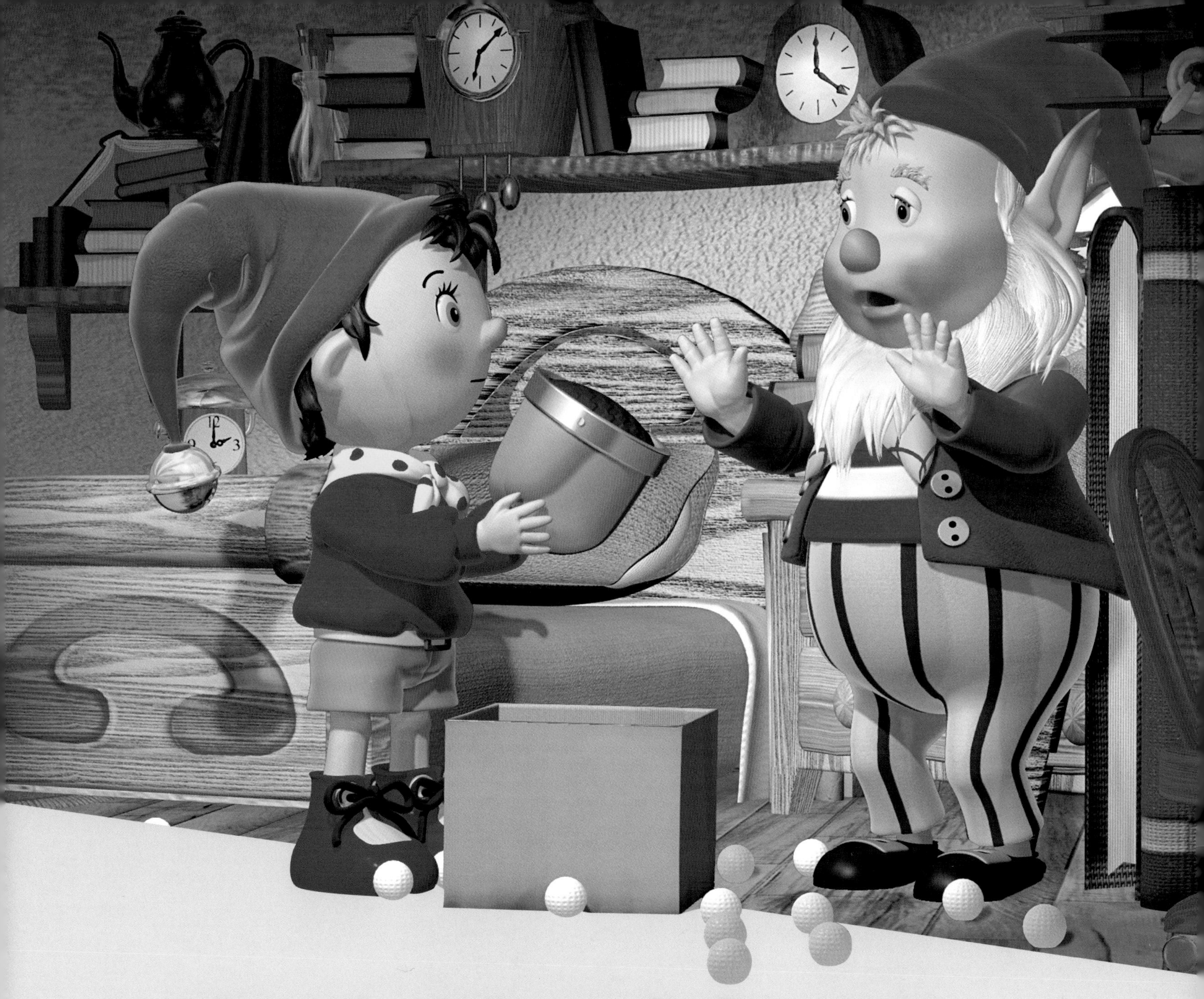

"What is that for?" asked Big-Ears, crossly.

"A car headlight for your moonlight, silly!" said Noddy. "Now *you* don't remember!"

"No, no, no, no, *no*!" cried Big-Ears. "I said a *torch*, not a *headlight*."

"Won't a headlight do?" asked Noddy.

"Well, at least I remembered the tool to make you snore!" said Noddy.

Big-Ears couldn't believe Noddy had been so silly. "I said *saw*, Noddy. Not *spanner*."

"Oh dear! What a bad memory I have," said Noddy. "But look, you could try this..." And he put the spanner on his nose.

Big-Ears pulled the spanner off Noddy's nose.

"I expect you've muddled up the flowers as well," sighed Big-Ears.

Noddy put his hand into the box and pulled out a bunch of dead weeds.

"Wrong!" groaned Big-Ears. "Just like everything else!"

“Noddy,” Big-Ears said sadly, “you didn’t remember one single thing.”

Noddy hung his head.

“I’m really sorry, Big-Ears,” he said. “I just don’t have a very good memory.”

Big-Ears smiled. "No, you don't. But you do have a good forgetery!"

Noddy sighed in relief. "Thank goodness you're not really cross, Big-Ears. I tried my best, truly I did."

"I know," said Big-Ears. "But if you need to remember something, write it down."

"What a good idea!" whooped Noddy, happily.

Big-Ears quickly wrote out a shopping list.

“Thanks,” said Noddy. “Now I’ll remember everything!” And he picked up the box and rushed downstairs.

Seconds later, he was back.

“Err… I forgot the list, Big-Ears,” he said, as he grabbed it.

Big-Ears grinned as he shuffled back to bed.

"That boy… Oops!" Big-Ears' foot slipped on a golf ball.

BOING! He hit the bed and then bounced up to the ceiling. THWACK! Down he came with a mighty THUD! Big-Ears was out cold!

A little while later, Noddy came back.

"I managed to get everything on the list!" he called. "Now you can get some sleep, Big-Ears. … oh!"

He stopped, staring in astonishment.

"Zzzz-zzzz-zzzz." Big-Ears was fast asleep, snoring loudly. He looked very comfortable.

Noddy crept over to the bed.

"Maybe you didn't need the sleeping charm after all," he whispered.

“Good night!” said Noddy, and he pulled the bedcovers gently over Big-Ears and tiptoed out.

“Zzzzzzzzzzzzzz…”

The Magic Powder

It was a sparkling spring morning in Toy Town…

"Ahh! What lovely weather!" sighed Mr Sparks. "It makes you want to sing and dance, doesn't it, Noddy?"

"It certainly does! I – oh, my goodness!"

All of a sudden, Noddy slammed on the brakes and jerked the steering wheel.

SCREEEECH! Noddy's little car skidded wildly before coming to a standstill sideways across the road.

Mr Sparks grabbed hold of his hat. Noddy's head shook so hard his bell tinkled madly.

"W-w-what happened?" gasped Mr Sparks, looking very startled.

"Sorry, Mr Sparks," said Noddy. "Something leaped out in front of the car. I only just missed it – Oh!"

"*Woof-woof-woof!*" Two paws and an eager nose appeared over the top of the car door.

"It's Bumpy Dog!" cried Mr Sparks. "And he's very happy to see you, Noddy!"

Bumpy barked and started licking Noddy's nose.

But Noddy wasn't very happy. "Bumpy! I nearly crashed into you! Get DOWN!"

"Don't be too hard on him," said Mr Sparks. "He's only a puppy. He doesn't understand about traffic rules."

Bumpy took a flying leap into the car.

But Noddy was still cross.

"You shouldn't run out in front of cars, Bumpy!" he scolded.

Bumpy Dog hung his head.

They were soon zooming along again towards Toy Town. Then, all of a sudden, Bumpy Dog jumped up at Noddy again.

"Get down at once, Bumpy!" shouted Noddy. "You should never, EVER mess about in a car!"

Bumpy whined. He hated it when Noddy was cross.

Poor Noddy. Something even worse was brewing in Dark Wood. The two bad goblins, Gobbo and Sly, were up to their usual tricks.

"Just two more things to add!" chortled Gobbo:

The sparkling laces of a ballerina's shoe,
The tapping rhythm of a drumstick true.
Dancing Potion, Dancing Potion,
Now you turn BLUE!

There was a FLASH! and the magic potion turned into sparkling blue powder.

Gobbo scooped up a handful. "Soon all of Toy Town will be dancing to our tune," he gloated.

"But Gobbo," whined Sly, "dancing's fun."

"They won't think it's fun when we've finished with them!" grinned Gobbo.

Soon Noddy stopped his car near Town Square.

"Thanks for the ride, Noddy," said Mr Sparks.

Bumpy was so excited that he jumped up again – and knocked Noddy over.

"Get DOWN!" Noddy cried. "Will you stop jumping and bumping all over the place?"

Poor Bumpy whined sadly and slunk away with his tail between his legs.

Just then, Noddy heard someone ringing a bell.

It was Gobbo the goblin.

"Roll up! Roll up!" yelled Gobbo. "Prepare to be AMAZED!"

What was Gobbo up to?

A crowd soon gathered to watch and Noddy joined them.

"No energy? Sore, aching feet?" cried Gobbo. "Never fear! I have here... a magic cure!"

And he waved towards a bottle full of sparkling blue powder.

"My Magic Comfort Foot Powder will put a spring in your step! You'll feel as if you're walking on air. One sprinkle and you'll be dancing in the streets!" Gobbo cried.

The Toy Town crowd murmured with surprise. Could they really trust Gobbo?

Just then, a stranger limped forward.

"Oooo, my feet are so-o-o sore," moaned the stranger. "I'd do anything to get rid of the pain."

"You won't be sorry, sir!" smirked Gobbo, as he pretended to sprinkle the powder over the stranger's feet.

"Wow!" Everyone gasped as the stranger leaped into the air and danced wildly across the stage.

The amazing dance convinced everyone.

"How much is that magic powder?" called out Mr Plod, the policeman.

"It's free… for one day only!" grinned Gobbo.

"It sounds too good to be true," said Noddy. "But I'll try some."

Soon, everyone had a bottle of Gobbo's Magic Comfort Foot Powder and they sprinkled the sparkling blue powder over their feet.

"Ooo, it feels lovely!" sighed Dinah Doll.

"Like I'm floating on air!" laughed Noddy.

Mr Plod smiled at Gobbo, "You've done something good for a change! Thank you!"

"Only too happy to help!" smirked Gobbo as the crowd walked away. The stranger stayed behind.

"Can I take off my disguise now, Gobbo?" he asked. It was Sly!

Gobbo laughed. "Of course you can, Sly! Heh! Heh! They fell for our trick! All those silly people tried our magic foot powder. Now we just need a little tune!"

Sly turned the handle of their music box and a lively tune filled the air. All at once, the goblins' Magic Comfort Foot Powder began to work its magic.

Feet began tapping and heads began nodding as everyone broke into a wild, crazy dance, twirling and whirling and spinning all around the town.

The two naughty goblins roared with laughter.

"It's the funniest thing I've ever seen," gasped Sly.

"Now's our chance," said Gobbo. "They can't stop us stealing – they're too busy dancing!"

At Dinah Doll's stall, poor Dinah could only dance and scold as Gobbo filled his sack.

"Don't worry, Dinah, I'll arrest them!" cried Mr Plod, dancing towards the two goblins.

"Oh, no you won't!" Gobbo sniggered, as the music played even faster. Mr Plod could do nothing but dance, dance, dance!

"HELP!" he wailed, whirling down the street.

The goblins' music had set Noddy's feet dancing and his head nodding too.

"What a nice car!" said Gobbo as he climbed into Noddy's car.

"You leave my car alone!" cried Noddy angrily.

"What's that, Noddy?" sniggered Gobbo. "Can't stop dancing? Never mind. We'll have your car."

The gleeful goblins loaded Noddy's car with everything they had stolen.

"There isn't one person in Toy Town who can stop us!" chortled Gobbo.

But he was wrong.

At that moment, Bumpy Dog wandered sadly into the square. But when he saw Noddy, he bounded happily up to him – and knocked him right over!

“Bumpy! Why aren’t you dancing?” cried Noddy, his feet still dancing in the air.

Bumpy barked.

“Of course!” Noddy laughed. “You don’t have any magic powder on your paws so you aren’t under the spell!”

He hugged Bumpy. “Now, go and stop those goblins!”

Bumpy leaped up at the two troublemakers and knocked the magic powder out of Gobbo's hands.

PUFF! A cloud of sparkling blue powder billowed out around them.

"Why, you pesky pooch, I'll – uh-oh!" Gobbo cried as his feet began to jiggle and wriggle.

Soon the two goblins were dancing furiously.

"Quick! Stop the music, Sly!" Gobbo shouted.

Sly stopped the music box and the goblins stopped dancing. But so did everyone else.

"Stop, in the name of Plod!" shouted the policeman as he ran towards them.

"Oops!" cried Gobbo. "You'd better start playing again, Sly!"

CRASH! Bumpy Dog knocked the music box out of Sly's hand and it smashed to pieces.

"Let's get out of here!" cried Gobbo. But it was too late!

Mr Plod grabbed both goblins. "Going somewhere?" he asked sternly.

"Heh, heh. To jail?" Sly said helpfully.

"You guessed it!" said Mr Plod.

"Well done, Bumpy, you're a hero!" said Dinah. "You deserve that bone for saving us from those naughty goblins."

"You're a great dog, Bumpy," cried Mr Sparks.

Then Bumpy bounded up to Noddy, wagging his tail like mad.

"I'm sorry I was mean to you, Bumpy," said Noddy. "Without all your jumping and bumping, we'd still be dancing to the goblins' tune! Are we still friends?"

Bumpy barked, leaped up at Noddy and… knocked him off his feet.

"Oh, Bumpy!" laughed Noddy.

Noddy the Rainbow Chaser

"We've done it, Tubby Bear," laughed Noddy and now I think we both deserve an ice-cream, don't you?"

And Master Tubby Bear had to agree.

SWOOSH!

Soon afterwards, Noddy and Tubby Bear were in the plane again – only this time, they were taking the pot of gold BACK to the Dark Wood.

The second that the pot hit the ground, the magic rainbow sprang back into the air, sparkling more brightly than ever over Toy Town.

Everyone felt terrible.

"Oh, no!" sniffed Tessie Bear. "I loved all those beautiful colours!"

"So did I," sighed Mr Wobbly Man.

"Don't be SAD!" cried Noddy. "I'll buy everyone an ice-cream!"

"I just want our rainbow back," said Tessie Bear.

"Oh, Big-Ears!" cried Noddy. "What can I do?"

"There is one thing you can do," said Big-Ears and he whispered in Noddy's ear.

Noddy nodded.

"Oh, dear!" said Big-Ears sadly. "That gold was put there by magic. It's what made the rainbow sparkle. Now it has been taken away, our wonderful rainbow has vanished for ever."

It was as if a big grey cloud had settled on Toy Town.

Everyone thought Noddy and Master Tubby Bear had been so brave.

"They're heroes!" cried Miss Pink Cat. Noddy smiled proudly, but Big-Ears frowned.

"Did the rainbow disappear when you took the pot of gold?" he asked.

"We've GOT THE GOLD!" whooped Noddy. Then, all of a sudden, the magic rainbow disappeared.

"Where did it go?" asked Master Tubby Bear.

"I don't know," said Noddy. "But one thing I DO know. Everyone is going to be very happy with us back in Toy Town!"

Noddy was a good pilot and he held the plane steady as it roared over the Dark Wood.

Closer and closer they got to the pot of gold until Master Tubby Bear could drop a rope to grab hold of it.

"But the treasure's just underneath us, Noddy," said Master Tubby Bear.

Noddy looked down from his plane and a very daring idea came into his head.

"Let's SCOOP it up, then. With the plane!"

A magic storm whistled through the trees and whirled them up into the air.

Round and round they tossed until the wind blew them back into Noddy's plane.

"Now I AM giving up," said Noddy. "Let's go home!"

Noddy and Master Tubby Bear fell to the ground and tumbled over and over.

"Whew!" said Noddy. "That was close!"

But they weren't safe yet.

The magic spell hadn't finished.

Noddy jumped up as high as he could and grabbed hold of Tubby Bear's shoes. Then he pulled and he pulled and he PULLED!

"He-e-elp!" squeaked Master Tubby Bear, as he slipped out of the grasp of the magic tree.

Poor Master Tubby Bear. The trees were coming alive. A long branch snatched him up and he was dangling in the air!

"Get me down!" yelled Tubby Bear.

All of a sudden, Tubby Bear felt someone tap him on the back.

"Is that you behind me, Noddy?" he quavered.

"I'm IN FRONT of you," said Noddy. "How can it be me?"

But then Noddy had a scary thought.

"Wait! Maybe there is a magic spell protecting the pot of gold. We'd better watch out!" he said.

Suddenly, there it was. The end of the rainbow. And there, on top of a hillock was a pot full of glittering GOLD!

"WE'VE FOUND THE TREASURE!" yelled Noddy.

And the friends did a little dance for joy.

“Follow me!” said Noddy, bravely.

Shimmering in the darkness, the magic rainbow stretched straight ahead. But fierce eyes winked at them through the gloom.

“I don’t like this ONE BIT,” grumbled Master Tubby Bear, running after his friend.

"Maybe I don't want that gold, after all," said Master Tubby Bear.

But Noddy wouldn't give up so easily. He landed the plane right in the middle of Dark Wood!

It didn't take the friends long to get ready and soon they were in the air.

"I can't WAIT to get that treasure," sighed Master Tubby Bear, happily.

But then Noddy saw where the rainbow was leading them... To the Dark Wood!

And Noddy sang a song:

Each of us would have a golden house
'Neath a silver tree.
What great fun for you and me
To be as rich as rich can be.

"So what are we waiting for? Let's follow that rainbow!"

Noddy took Master Tubby Bear to find the Toy Town plane.

"The goblins were right about one thing. It WOULD be nice to have all that gold," said Tubby Bear.

"That's why we're going on a treasure hunt – at the end of the magic rainbow!" said Noddy.

Noddy looked thoughtful.

"Oh, Noddy!" said Master Tubby Bear. "Do you really believe that story about the pot of gold?"

"Come with me, Tubby Bear," grinned Noddy. "I've just had a brilliant idea!"

"Oh, no you won't!" said Mr Plod. "Because you're going to the police station, right now. Miss Pink Cat tells me you've been after her pies again!" And he whisked the grumbling goblins away.

Just then, the naughty goblins arrived. "Huh! Happy!" sneered Gobbo. "Who cares? There's a big pot of gold at the end of that rainbow."

"And when we find it WE'LL be happy!" said Sly. "Cos we'll be RICH!"

"It's a magic rainbow, Noddy," said Big-Ears. "So it doesn't need rain. It just turns up when it feels like it."

"And makes everyone happy," added Miss Pink Cat. "I know, because it's been coming ever since I was a Pink Kitten!"

“It’s so beautiful!” cried Tessie Bear. “Look at the yellow.”

“Look at the orange,” mewed Miss Pink Cat.

“And this red!” said Mr Wobbly Man.

“I love all the colours!” smiled Noddy. “But it hasn’t rained. So where has this rainbow come from?”

It was a special day in Toy Town. A magic rainbow was sparkling in the sky over Town Square. Everyone was very excited.